It's Rhyme Time!

By
Betsy Flikkema

Cover Illustration by
Roberta Collier-Morales
Inside Illustrations by
Janet Armbrust

Publisher
Carson-Dellosa Publishing Company, Inc.
Greensboro, North Carolina

Dedication:
To Isabel Rose
who clapped and sang and danced with me
through the writing of this book.

Credits:
Author: Elizabeth Flikkema
Cover Illustration: Roberta Collier-Morales
Inside Illustrations: Janet Armbrust
Project Director: Sherrill B. Flora
Editors: Sherrill B. Flora, Karen Seberg, Sharon Thompson
Graphic Layout: Gray House Graphics

ISBN: 0-88724-916-7

Table of Contents

Alphabet Letters

Great A, Little A

As you say this rhyme, act out the word that goes with the letter. For example, arms overhead for great A and crouch down for a little a. You may decide the motions or ask the children to help you.

Great A, little a, bouncing b, c is cool, and d dandy.
Big E, fancy f, graceful g. H is hot and I icy.
Small j, jumpy J, kicking k. L is late and m just may.
Nice n, open o, prancing p. Q is quiet and r rowdy.
Small s, tiny t, ugly u. V is vanishing with w.
Next one, little x, yawning y. Z is at the door, saying bye.

(Alternatively, this has a nice rhythm for clapping patterns, such as clap hands, clap your partner's right hand, clap hands, clap your partner's left hand, clap hands, clap both of your partner's hands, clap hands.)

Letter-Day Rhyme

On letter days, as students bring in objects that begin with the letter, sing this song to the tune of "Skip to My Lou." Substitute the letter of the day for T in the song. Sing the song once for each object the children bring in. Replace the word tiger with the name of the object as you hold it up.

T, T, what starts with T?
Tuh, tuh, what starts with tuh?   *(use letter sound—not letter name—here)*
T, T, what starts with T?
Tiger starts with T.

Capital Letter Song

This song is simple but will help remind children to start from the top when forming their capital letters. Speak in the rhythm of "Pat-a-Cake."

Alphabet, alphabet, ABCs.
Learning the letters from A to Z.
Start at the top
Go down on the left.
Forming the capitals, one at a time.

Baseball

I Love Baseball

Sing to the tune of "Are You Sleeping?"
Have students echo you; or split the class into two parts for call and response.

I love baseball, I love baseball.
Hit that ball, hit that ball.
Let's play at the ballpark. Let's play at the ballpark.
Baseball game, baseball game.

Do Your Duty

Pitcher, pitcher, do your duty.   *(pretend to throw a ball)*
Throw this ball; an American beauty.   *(salute)*
Pitch it fast and pitch it true.   *(flick thumb up from index finger)*
Strike him (or her) out 'cause we love you. *(criss-cross arms on chest)*

Watch Our Faces

Recite this rhyme while waiting in line or trying to get everybody's attention. Students must watch you to see if you give the "safe" or "out" sign. The sign you give determines how they react in the final line.

Hit the ball.   *(pretend to bat)*
Run the bases.   *(arms make running circles)*
Make the call.   *(make either the safe call or the out call with your hands)*
And watch our faces.   *(students' faces and bodies—but not voices—reflect the call)*

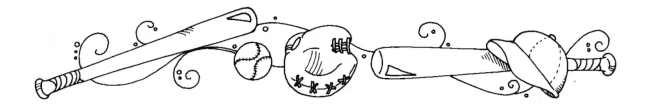

Beach/Ocean

Five Little Crabs

This counting rhyme is great for a beach theme or ocean animals theme. Use the crab pattern below to make either five puppets or five felt crabs. Copy the words of the rhyme on five pages (one line per page) for the children to illustrate and make books to read and take home.

Five little crabs playing on the shore. One skittered off and then there were four.
Four little crabs feeling safe and free. One saw a snack and then there were three.
Three little crabs wondered what to do. One caught a wave and then there were two.
Two little crabs basking in the sun. One got too hot and then there was one.
One little crab feeling all alone, slipped in the water . . . and all the crabs were home.

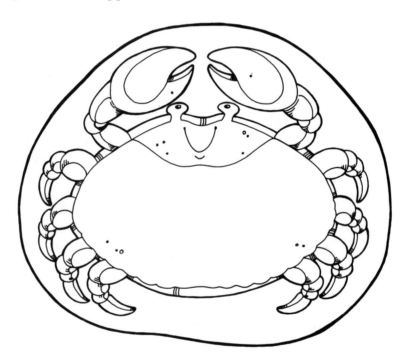

Tongue Twister

Say this as a call-and-response rhyme. One group or individual says the first line and a second group or individual says the second. Children will have fun repeating this and taking turns saying the different lines.

She sells seashells by the seashore.
"Seashells for sale! Seven cents a shell!"

Carly Barley at the Beach

*After learning this rhyme, ask students to draw what Carly Barley looks like
(perhaps a huge Dr. Seuss-like bird sitting stubbornly).*

Carly Barley sat on a dune.   *(arms crossed)*

Carly Barley stayed there past noon.   *(forearm straight up, resting elbow on back of other hand)*

Neither chocolate nor cakes, nor money or more   *(hand to mouth and then rub fingers together)*

Could coax Carly off that sand by the shore.   *(pull index fingers toward you)*

Swan Song

This is a Mother Goose rhyme with a finger play. Have students stand up so they can swim away and back.

Swan swam over the sea   *(make swan's head with clasped hands; your arms are its long neck; move forward)*

Swim, swan, swim!   *(dog paddle)*

Swan swam back again,   *(make swan's head with clasped hands; your arms are its long neck; move backward)*

Well swum, swan!   *(clap for swan)*

Body

How Many Friends?

Students hold up their fingers as they count the number of friends named.

How many friends have I got?
Let's count the whole silly lot.
There's Kathy and Lena who like to dress up,
Matthew and Nathan who slurp their teacup.
Philip and Andrew and Marjie and Leigh,
Who all like to sit in the tepee and read.
And finally Allie and Peter, the best!
My friends who NEVER like to rest.
Some people may think that's a lot,
But ten is the number of friends that I've got.

(wiggle your fingers in front of your face)

Peter's Lunch

While you read this active story, the students act out the motions that go with the noises.

It was time for lunch.
Peter's mother couldn't find him.
She went outside and called and called.
Soon she heard two little hands go clap, clap, clap.
The noise came from inside the house.
Then she heard two little feet go stomp, stomp, stomp.
The noise came from the hall.
Next, she heard two little hands go wash, wash, wash.
Mother knew where Peter was.
Then she heard one little body go sit, sit, sit.
Peter must be in the kitchen.
She heard a little chair go scrape, scrape, scrape.
There was Peter at the table.
One hungry boy went slurp, slurp, slurp.

Five Senses

Sing to the tune of "This Little Light of Mine."

This little mouth of mine, it's gonna taste what's sweet.
　　(touch fingers on one hand to mouth and open hand)
These two eyes of mine, they're gonna see so well.
　　(index fingers on eyes then point out)
These two ears on the side, they're gonna hear you speak.
　　(cup hands around ears)
I'm gonna taste, see, and hear my world.
　　(touch mouth, eyes, ears, and open arms)

These two hands of mine, they can touch and feel.
　　(wiggle fingers)
This small nose of mine, it can smell so fine.
　　(touch nose and bring hand out)
These five senses of mine, they have great appeal.
　　(hold up five fingers)
I'm gonna feel, gonna smell, my world.
　　(wiggle fingers, touch nose, open arms)

Body Patterns

Using the AAABB pattern, have the children do the actions as you say the pattern.
After doing those given here, invite the children to come up with different body motions.

Clap, clap, clap	*(clap three times)*	Shake, shake, shake	*(shake hands out)*
Stomp, stomp	*(stomp feet)*	Smack, smack	*(smack lips twice)*
Clap, clap, clap		Shake, shake, shake	
Stomp, stomp		Smack, smack	

Hear, hear, hear	*(touch ears three times)*	Knee, knee, knee	*(tap knees three times)*
Wiggle, wiggle	*(wiggle body)*	Nod, nod	*(nod head)*
Hear, hear, hear		Knee, knee, knee	
Wiggle, wiggle		Nod, nod	

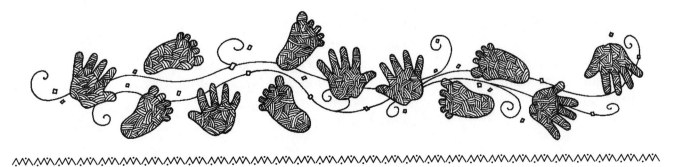

Let's Wash

Play music while the children use their hands to pretend they are washing. Allow about fifteen seconds for children to act out what you say.

Let's wash our faces.
Let's wash our hands.
Let's wash our feet.
Let's wash our backs.
Let's wash our knees.
Let's wash our elbows.
Let's wash our ears.
Let's wash our hair.
Let's wash all over.

I'm Growing

By anonymous

There's something about me that I'm knowing.
    (squat on the ground; point to forehead and
  tap)
There's something about me that isn't showing.
    (still squatting; shake head)
I'm GROWING!!!!
    (jump up and shout this line)

Ten Fingers

By anonymous

I have ten little fingers,	*(hold up ten fingers)*
And they all belong to me.	*(put hands together by chest)*
I can make them do things.	*(make hands do a variety of movements)*
Would you like to see?	*(touch index fingers to eyes)*
I can shut them up tight,	*(make fists)*
Or open them wide.	*(stretch fingers out wide)*
I can put them together,	*(place palm to palm)*
Or make them all hide.	*(put hands behind your back)*
I can make them jump high,	*(open hands alternately, go up above head)*
I can make them jump low,	*(move curled fingers a little up and down)*
I can fold them quietly,	*(fold hands in front of chest)*
And hold them just so.	*(bring folded hands to lap)*

Bugs

Creepy Spiders

Use the finger motions or act out the story. Make a large web with string on the floor.
Assign roles to the children. Several children can say the lines of the mama and dad. Copy
and color the tree and spiders on page 12. Attach the spiders to the tree with removable
tape. Tape the tree to the chalkboard. As you read the story, remove one spider at a time.

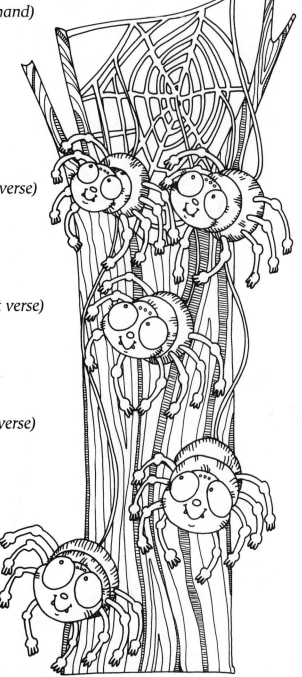

Five creepy spiders playing on a tree,
   (show five fingers, then wiggle four fingers on each hand)
One eats a bug and falls fast asleep.
   (clap hands then make a pillow on cheek for sleep)
"Yum," says its mama. "Yum," says its dad.
   (rub tummy)
Poor little bug, that's too bad.
   (shake head sadly)

Four creepy spiders playing on a tree,
   (show four fingers and repeat finger plays from first verse)
One eats a bug and falls fast asleep.
"Yum," says its mama. "Yum," says its dad.
Poor little bug, that's too bad.

Three creepy spiders playing on a tree,
   (show three fingers and repeat finger plays from first verse)
One eats a bug and falls fast asleep.
"Yum," says its mama. "Yum," says its dad.
Poor little bug, that's too bad.

Two creepy spiders playing on a tree,
   (show two fingers and repeat finger plays from first verse)
One eats a bug and falls fast asleep.
"Yum," says its mama. "Yum," says its dad.
Poor little bug, that's too bad.

One creepy spider playing on a tree,
   (show one finger then wiggle four
   fingers on each hand)
It eats a bug and shouts "Owee!"
   (wiggling fingers clap together)
"Pardon?" says its mama. "What?" says its dad.
   (hand by right ear, then left ear)
"That bug messed my web and I'm really mad!"
   (shake finger)

Follow the directions on page 11.

Spiders and Insects

Spiders have eight legs.   *(wiggle four fingers on each hand)*
Insects have six.   *(wiggle three fingers on each hand)*
Insects have two wings   *(use hands as wings)*
To get away quick.   *(make hands fly up and away)*

The Eency Weency Spider

You can add your own verses to this fun rhyme. Where might the spider try to climb at school?

The eency weency spider went up the water spout.
    (put index fingers to thumbs alternately to make a climbing motion)
Down came the rain and washed the spider out.
    (wiggle ten fingers down from sky and move open hands side to side)
Out came the sun and dried up all the rain
    (arms in circle overhead)
And the eency weency spider went up the spout again.
    (fingers climb again)

The eency weency spider went up the kitchen chair.
    (fingers climb up)
Down came a leg and knocked it out of there.
    (bring fist down)
Dinnertime was over and all the chairs pushed in.
    (wipe hands together and push an imaginary chair in)
And the eency weency spider climbed up with a big grin.
    (fingers climb up, then fingers at corners of smile)

The eency weency spider went up the telephone cord.
    (fingers climb up)
Ring went the phone and scared him out of his gourd.
    (hands snap open on both sides of head)
When the call was finished, the phone went back in place.
    (pretend to put telephone receiver back in cradle)
And the eency weency spider was gone without a trace.
    (fingers start to climb up, then hands open out, palms up)

Ladybug

Is a ladybug a lady?
There must be some big lug
Who would prefer it if we called him
A big red gentleman bug.

Black and Yellow Bees

Copy and cut out the bee patterns on page 15 to use with this rhyme. This counting rhyme could be adapted for practicing tens. In that case, start with fifty bees and have ten take a dive.

Five black and yellow bees
Finding nectar in flowers and trees.
One took a dive into the hive.
Now there were four searching bees.

Four black and yellow bees
Finding nectar in flowers and trees.
One took a dive into the hive.
Now there were three searching bees.

Three black and yellow bees
Finding nectar in flowers and trees.
One took a dive into the hive.
Now there were two searching bees.

Two black and yellow bees
Finding nectar in flowers and trees.
One took a dive into the hive.
Now there was one searching bee.

One black and yellow bee
Finding nectar in flowers and trees.
He took a dive into the hive.
Now there were no searching bees.

Shoo Fly

Shoo fly, don't bother me.
    (wiggle fingers and have them fly, then push away with hand)
Shoo fly, don't bother me.
    (repeat motions)
Shoo fly, don't bother me.
    (repeat motions)
I belong to somebody.
    (point to self; hug self)

Use with the rhyme, "Black and Yellow Bees," found on page 14.

Colors

Copy the furry monster on page 17 on yellow, orange, green, and red paper. Give each child one or two colors. As the color is mentioned in the poem, the children hold up the correctly colored monster. As they listen, invite them to guess the color before it is mentioned.

Once there was a furry monster feeling rather brave.
Thought he'd go exploring though he'd never left his cave.
His mother always warned him to stay away from light.
Today was the day he'd find out that she was right!

He walked out slowly that happy little fellow.
The sun shone bright in a lovely shade of yellow.
He looked right up into that friendly sun.
What a surprise when yellow he'd become!

Then he found some oranges hanging on a tree.
He ate those tasty fruits, and happy now was he.
Until he noticed with a feeling of dread,
His furry body was orange from his feet to his head.

Tired from the changes, the monster took a break.
He rested in the green leaves by the gentle lake.
As he slept, he felt rather keen,
And when he woke, he was a brilliant green.

Now the sun was setting and in the sky was low;
The monster's day was done, and it was time to go.
Just as the sun was changing, the monster turned his head,
The sunset glowed, and the monster turned bright red.

Furry Monster

Follow the directions on page 16.

Red

Red sky at night, sailors' delight.
Red sky in morning, sailors take warning.

Blue

Blue sky, blue,
The sun will shine all day.
Blue night, bright,
The moon and stars will stay.

Yellow

The yellow sun is shining, shining, shining.
The yellow sun is shining
Whatever shall we do?

Green

When in the trees the leaves are green,
Birds and butterflies will be seen.

Purple

Of purple and lavender, I shall sing.
I shall be queen and you shall be king.

Orange

Sweet oranges in January and pumpkins in fall,
Many things with orange color are shaped like a ball.

Black and White

Black and white are partner colors.
They are the best of friends.
Made of no color and every color,
Not found where the rainbow bends.

Days of the Week

Days of the Week

Sing to the tune of "Yankee Doodle."

Sunday Monday Tuesday Wednesday Thursday Friday Saturday,
When Sunday comes around again, repeat them with a friend.

Morning Song

Sing to the tune of "The More We Get Together." Substitute the correct day for Monday. Sing the subsequent four days in line three.

I'm glad we're here on Monday, on Monday, on Monday.
I'm glad we're here on Monday, one day of the week.
        Next comes Tuesday and Wednesday and Thursday and Friday.
I'm glad we're here on Monday, one day of the week.

Come to My Party

This rhyme has a verse to recite each day of the week. Or, recite a verse on birthdays or approaching holidays. The finger play uses American Sign Language for some key words.

Will you come to my party, will you come? *(pull index fingers toward you, make a sign for P on both hands and shake them in front of you)*

We'll all have candy and bubble gum. *(twist index finger into cheek, then bend two fingers into cheek)*

All your friends will be there. *(hook index fingers together and reverse)*
Bring a toy you can share. *(bring fists down together from shoulders)*
Will you come on Monday, will you come? *(sign letter M and move it in a circle)*

Will you come to my party, will you come? *(pull index fingers toward you, make a sign for P on both hands and shake them in front of you)*

Be ready to dance, whistle, and hum. *(point two fingers over your open palm and swing them)*

We will play a new game. *(bring fists down together from shoulders)*
If you miss it, what a shame! *(tap forehead with fist)*
Will you come on Tuesday, will you come? *(sign letter T and move it in a circle)*

∧∧∧∧∧∧∧∧∧∧∧∧∧∧∧∧∧∧∧∧∧∧∧∧∧∧∧∧∧∧∧∧∧∧∧∧∧∧

Will you come to my party, will you come?

(pull index fingers toward you, make a sign for P on both hands and shake them in front of you)

The food will make you say "Yum!" *(rub tummy)*

Dress up like a bear *(cross arms in front of yourself and scratch)*

Or a lion if you dare. *(make a claw on your forehead and pull it zig-zag back through your hair—like a mane)*

Will you come on Wednesday, will you come? *(sign letter W and move it in a circle)*

Will you come to my party, will you come?

(pull index fingers toward you, make a sign for P on both hands and shake them in front of you)

Come whether there is rain or sun. *(wave hands up and down; sign the letter C around your eye)*

Lots of balloons of blue *(sign the letter B and shake it)*

Will be there for you. *(point at someone)*

Will you come on Thursday, will you come? *(sign letter H and move it in a circle)*

Will you come to my party, will you come?

(pull index fingers toward you, make a sign for P on both hands and shake them in front of you)

Bring your own peach or a plum. *(put hand to mouth and snap outward)*

We'll eat chocolate cake *(tap mouth with fingers)*

And have crafts to make. *(sign letter C with both hands and move back and forth in front of chest)*

Will you come on Friday, will you come? *(sign letter F and move it in a circle)*

Will you come to my party, will you come?

(pull index fingers toward you, make a sign for P on both hands and shake them in front of you)

On Saturday, we will have lots of fun. *(sign letter S and move it in a circle)*

Then Sunday we will rest *(move open hands in a circle)*

For we had been blessed *(touch lips with fingertips; move down to open hand)*

To a week of parties, you did come. *(make a sign for P on both hands and shake them in front of you)*

∧∧∧∧∧∧∧∧∧∧∧∧∧∧∧∧∧∧∧∧∧∧∧∧∧∧∧∧∧∧∧∧∧∧∧∧∧∧

Sunday Comes on Silent Wings

Cut out the penguins on page 22 to use during your class calendar time.

Sunday comes on silent wings,
　　(make wings with arms)
Monday bright and sunny sings.
　　(form sun over head with arms)
Tuesday brings something new,
　　(hold index finger and thumb at temples and flick index finger up)
Wednesday is midweek for you.
　　(sign the letter W and circle it around)
Thursday is a day to help a friend,
　　(hook index fingers one way and then the other)
Friday starts the weekend.
　　(sign the letter F and circle it around)
Saturday is full of fun and games;
　　(bring fists down together from shoulders)
Can you give all weekday names?
　　(hold up seven fingers)

Limerick

There once was a penguin who could speak.
He knew all the days of the week.
He said them of course,
Until he was hoarse.
Now all he can make is a squeak.

*Copy, color and cut out the penguin
patterns found on page 22. Use the penguins
to sequence the days of the week.*

December Holidays

Reindeer

Expend some of that holiday energy with this active rhyme. You can sing it to the tune of "Twinkle, Twinkle."

Reindeer, reindeer, feet so light,   *(prance around the circle)*
Please be careful in your flight.   *(hold arms out in flight)*
You all have so far to go   *(point ahead)*
All across the world, I know.   *(arms make a big circle)*
Reindeer, reindeer, feet so light,   *(prance around the circle)*
Please come safely home tonight.   *(stop prancing and sit down)*

Celebration of the Lights

Sing to the tune of "Sukey Put the Kettle On."

Papa, light the candle, now.   *(touch the tip of one finger)*
Papa, light the candle, now.   *(touch the tip of a second finger)*
Papa, light the candle, now.   *(touch the tip of a third finger)*
With hope and peace.   *(make peace sign with two fingers)*

Dreidel Song

Sing to the tune of "Sukey, Put the Kettle On."

Brother, spin the dreidel, now.   *(make spinning motion with index finger)*
Brother, spin the dreidel, now.
Brother, spin the dreidel, now.
We'll play all night.   *(rest cupped hand on the back of opposite hand)*

Little Jack Horner

Little Jack Horner sat in a corner,   *(for little, hold finger and thumb close;*
Sat in a corner.   *make a corner with fingertips together)*
Eating his Christmas pie;   *(pretend to eat)*
He put in his thumb,   *(put thumb down)*
And pulled out a plum,   *(turn thumb up)*
And said, "What a good boy am I!"   *(hook thumbs under arms)*

Dinosaurs

Dinosaur

This rhyme is a loud-to-quiet rhyme, which is great for the times you need to calm the group down before starting a quiet activity.

There was a big dinosaur	*(bend three fingers on each hand in front of chest and alternate them up and down two times)*
Went stomping through the land.	*(pound fists on knees)*
He pitter-patted through the leaves,	*(lightly tap hands on knees)*
And tip-toed through the sand.	*(fingers walk on knees)*
He walked and ate and watched for you	*(tap mouth with fingers)*
But didn't see a clue.	*(hand over eyes—looking)*
Millions of years—silent were his feet.	*(index finger to lips)*
Now we watch for clues,	*(index finger and thumb draw a*
And wish that we could meet.	*line down in front of chest)*

Dinosaurs, Dinosaurs

Recite and use finger plays or divide the class and chant the lines responsively.

Dinosaurs, dinosaurs,	*(bend three fingers on each hand in front of chest*
We love you a bunch.	*and alternate them up and down two times)*
Meat eaters, plant eaters,	*(criss-cross arms across chest)*
What did you munch?	*(bring four fingers forward and back in front of mouth)*
Jurassic, Jurassic,	*(bend three fingers on each hand in front of chest*
Apatosaurus.	*and alternate them up and down two times)*
Long ago, long ago,	*(touch imaginary watch)*
You never knew us!	
Cretaceous, Cretaceous,	*(bend three fingers on each hand in front of chest*
Tyrannosaurus Rex.	*and alternate them up and down two times)*
How were you colored?	*(wiggle four fingers on your chin)*
Stripes or spots or checks?	

Ten Hungry Dinosaurs

Count on your fingers as you sing this song to the tune of "Ten Little Indians." Use the patterns on pages 25 and 26 to create a finger puppet for each number.

One hungry, two hungry, three hungry dinosaurs,
Four hungry, five hungry, six hungry dinosaurs,
Seven hungry, eight hungry, nine hungry dinosaurs,
Eating in the swamp.

Follow directions on page 24.

Follow directions on page 24.

Earth

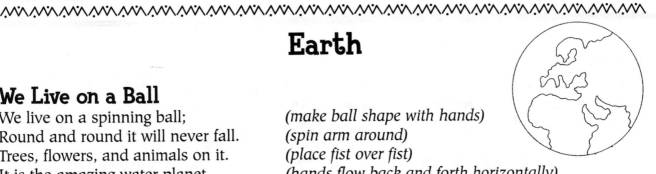

We Live on a Ball

We live on a spinning ball;   *(make ball shape with hands)*
Round and round it will never fall.   *(spin arm around)*
Trees, flowers, and animals on it.   *(place fist over fist)*
It is the amazing water planet.   *(hands flow back and forth horizontally)*

Ours to Share

Sing to the tune of "The Farmer in the Dell."

The earth is ours to share.
The earth is ours to share.
Take care of things that live on earth.
The earth is ours to share.

Earth Keepers

Take good care of the earth.   *(hold one fist in the other near heart)*
Keep it clean for all it's worth.   *(pretend to pick up trash)*
It is your job and mine   *(point to you and me)*
To make sure it is fine.   *(pat your own back)*
Take good care of the earth.   *(hold one fist in the other near heart)*

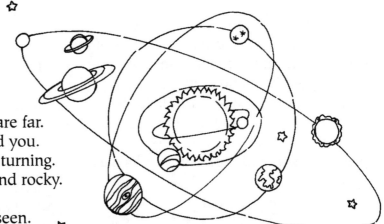

Nine Planets

Nine planets spin 'round a star.
Mercury is close; Pluto and Neptune are far.
The Earth is blue and home to me and you.
Venus is burning; Saturn with rings is turning.
Jupiter is big and cocky; Mars is red and rocky.
Uranus is cold and looks green.
These are the planets scientists have seen.

Earth Day

Trees lush, rivers bright, (*arms form branches, then sun overhead*)
Natural things on earth delight. (*pull a growing thing from your palm*)
For animals and birds I fight, (*fingers on chest; bend hands, then make a beak with one hand in front of your mouth*)

And hope that all will be all right. (*touch lips with fingers, then bring open hand down to opposite open hand*)

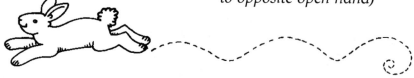

All Things Natural

This poem can be spoken or sung to the tune of "For Health and Strength." Children are born naturalists. They are very sincere about their love of natural things.

For animals both big and small, we pledge our help and care.
Under oak and pine and ash and fir, we find our shelter there.
In fields and streams, and mountains tall, the animals find their homes.
We are in charge of living space; let's care for all biomes.
Trees, animals, and people too, all need clean, healthy air.
We must be careful with the earth; don't take more than your share.

I See the Trees

We are bound to the earth and everything in it. This is a celebration of appreciation for that relationship.

I see the trees, and the trees see me. (*open hand twists back and forth*)
I take care of trees, and they take care of me.
I see the birds, and the birds see me. (*open hand by mouth like a beak*)
I protect the birds, and they please me.
I love the earth, and the earth loves me. (*middle finger and thumb touch back of*
I support the earth, and the earth supports me. *opposite hand; move the hand up and down*)
I see trash, and the trash bothers me. (*pretend to wrinkle paper in hands*)
I pick up trash, and the earth thanks me.

Food

I'm a Little Apple

Sing to the tune of "I'm a Little Teapot."

I'm a little apple, sweet and red.
   (arms up with fingers touching the top of your head, then twist index fingers on each cheek)
Here is my round shape.   *(arms out with fingertips on hips)*
Here is my stem.   *(one arm over head)*
Sideways down my middle, cut me please.   *(cut with hand at abdomen)*
Deep inside a star of seeds
   (make starburst by putting all ten fingers together and opening hands quickly palms out)

The Fruit in my Mouth

Sing to the tune of "The Wheels on the Bus."

The bananas in my mouth go mush, mush, mush,
mush, mush, mush,   *(rub hands together)*
mush, mush, mush.
The bananas in my mouth go mush, mush, mush,
Eating all my fruit.
   Other verses:
Apples in my mouth go crunch, crunch, crunch.   *(pound fists together)*
Grapes in my mouth go squish, squish, squish.   *(pinch fingers)*
Lemons in my mouth go pucker, pucker, pucker.   *(make a pucker mouth)*
Watermelon in my mouth goes slurp, slurp, slurp.   *(hands catch splashes out of mouth)*
Strawberries in my mouth go yum, yum, yum.   *(rub tummy)*

Nutrition

Sing to the tune of "Pop Goes the Weasel."
Bread, milk, vegetables, and meat,
Along with fruit and water.
Mix it up each day to eat.
Yum! A healthy diet!

Crunch Down

Sing to the tune of "My Bonnie Lies over the Ocean."

Crunch down and eat up your carrots,
Crunch down and eat up your peas.
Crunch down and eat up your veggies;
Eat up all your veggies today!

Crunch down, eat up;
Eat up your veggies, today, today!
Crunch down, eat up;
Oh, eat up your veggies today!

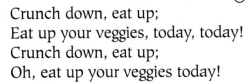

29

Underground

Carrots, turnips, onions, too,   *(crying with fists wiping eyes)*
Grow as beets and potatoes do.   *(place fist over fist)*
Leaves growing up, roots shooting down.   *(hands come together and separate*
                                          as they move up, then opposite for roots)

Dig up veggies from the ground.   *(digging motion)*

Peanut Butter and Jelly Train

Designate three fourths of the class to say "peanut butter" repeatedly like the "choo-choo-choo" of a train.

The other children wait for your cue to say "jel-ly" like the "whoo-oo" whistle of the train. Repeat the pattern of four or five peanut butters to one jelly several times. After practice, you can teach the children to slow the "pea-nut but-ter"s to sound like the train is slowing down.

Macaroni and Cheese

I like macaroni and cheese.
I don't like spinach or broccoli or peas.
Please, no celery crunch.
I won't eat nuggets for lunch.
My mom makes me eat
Lentils, tofu, and meat.
But I like macaroni and cheese.

Snack Time

Encourage your students to make healthy choices for snack time. Sing to the tune of "Twinkle, Twinkle."

Snack time, snack time, time to eat.   *(clap four times and touch your watch)*
Wash your hands and have a treat.   *(rub hands, pretend to eat)*
Cheese and crackers, pretzels, ham.   *(count on fingers)*
Carrots, celery, yogurt, jam.   *(count on fingers)*
Snack time, snack time, healthy treat.   *(clap four times, rub tummy)*
There are lots of snacks to eat.   *(rub hands, pretend to eat)*

PIZZA

Sing to the tune of "BINGO."

There was a baker had some dough,   *(place fist over fist)*
Tomato sauce, and cheese.
P-I-Z-Z-A, P-I-Z-Z-A, P-I-Z-Z-A   *(clap hands with each letter as you spell)*
And pizza he did make.   *(rub tummy)*

He took that dough and rolled it out,   *(roll out dough)*
And formed it into crust.
P-I-Z-Z-A, P-I-Z-Z-A, P-I-Z-Z-A   *(clap hands with each letter as you spell)*
And pizza he did make.   *(rub tummy)*

He poured on sauce and sprinkled cheese, *(wiggle fingers as sprinkling)*
And baked it in the oven.
P-I-Z-Z-A, P-I-Z-Z-A, P-I-Z-Z-A   *(clap hands with each letter as you spell)*
And pizza he did make.   *(rub tummy)*

When cheese was melted, pizza done,   *(roll pizza cutter)*
He cut it into slices.
P-I-Z-Z-A, P-I-Z-Z-A, P-I-Z-Z-A   *(clap hands with each letter as you spell)*
And pizza we did eat.   *(stretch cheese up from mouth)*

Forest Animals

The Birds in the Tree

Sung this song to the tune of "The Wheels on the Bus." Have the students choose the animals and actions or sounds. Copy, color and cut out the patterns found on page 33. Hold up the animals as you sing each verse.

The birds in the tree go tweet, tweet, tweet,
　　　(hands in front of mouth like a beak opening and shutting)
tweet, tweet, tweet,
tweet, tweet, tweet.
The birds in the tree go tweet, tweet, tweet,
Fluttering to their nests.

The squirrels in the tree go up and down,　*(raise body up and down)*
up and down,
up and down.
The squirrels in the tree go up and down,
Frisking 'round the yard.

The worms on the tree go wiggle, wiggle, wiggle,
　　　(hold hands and forearms together and wiggle them)
wiggle, wiggle, wiggle,
wiggle, wiggle, wiggle.
The worms on the tree go wiggle, wiggle, wiggle,
Searching for good food.

The rabbits 'neath the tree go dig, dig, dig,　*(pretend to shovel dirt)*
dig, dig, dig,
dig, dig, dig.
The rabbits 'neath the tree go dig, dig, dig,
Tunneling in the roots.

Directions found on page 32.

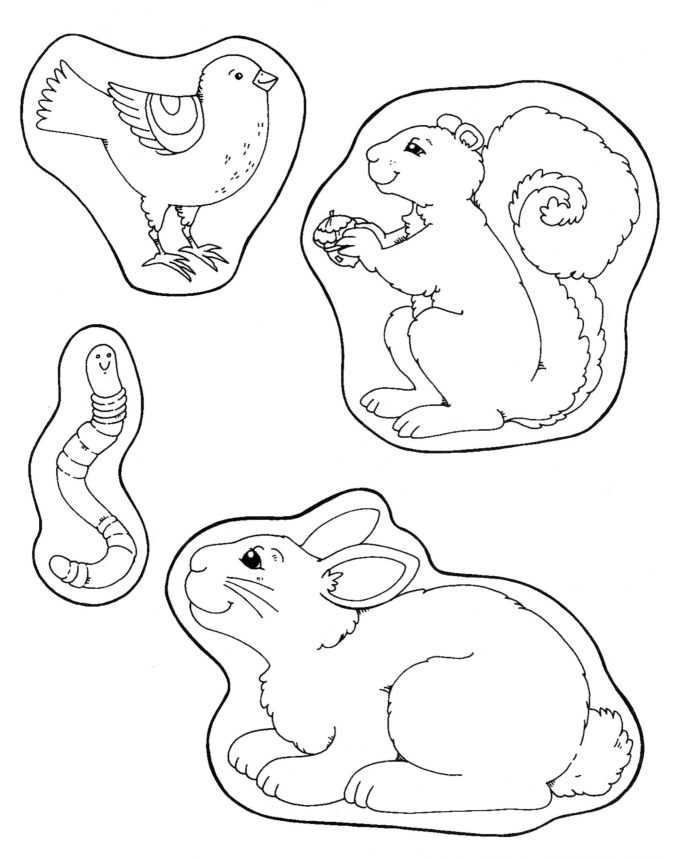

Friends

New Kid

There once was a new girl at school.
She worried that kids would be cruel.
She smiled and said,
"Will you be my friend?"
That's all it took to be cool.

Two Best Friends

This song counts up rather than down, encouraging students to build more friendships.
Sung to the tune of "Five Fat Turkeys Are We."

Two best friends are we.	*(show two fingers)*
We play all day till three.	*(point pinkies and thumbs and twist hands)*
We're always together,	*(make a big hug)*
Whatever the weather.	*(fingers rain down)*
Won't you join us, please?	*(circle tummy with flat hand)*
Three best friends are we.	*(show three fingers)*
We play all day till three.	*(point pinkies and thumbs and twist hands)*
We're always together,	*(make a big hug)*
Whatever the weather.	*(fingers rain down)*
Won't you join us, please?	*(circle tummy with flat hand)*

Four best friends are we . . .
Five best friends are we . . .

What Is a Friend?

A friend is someone you know,	*(hook index fingers one way; then reverse)*
Over time, together you grow.	*(raise hand up, palm down)*
A friend is someone you trust,	*(criss-cross arms in front of body)*
Never leaves you behind in the dust.	*(uncross arms and bring them slowly down to sides)*
Everyone here is your friend,	*(hook index fingers one way; then reverse)*
As time together you spend.	*(touch imaginary watch)*
When trouble comes by,	*(look over shoulder)*
Friends won't let you cry.	*(rub eyes)*
So be gentle with friends always,	*(hook index fingers one way; then reverse)*
They'll be with you all of your days.	*(point up and set elbow on your fingertips, bring the pointing finger down to rest on opposite arm)*

Best Friend

Sung to the tune of "Yankee Doodle."

My best friend likes riding bikes,
And my best friend likes walking.
The only thing that I don't get
Is my best friend likes broccoli.
Playing, playing with my friend,
Playing games and dress-up.
We don't like things all the same,
But we like each other.

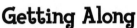

Getting Along

Preschool children need lots of reminders to use words rather than crying or hitting to solve problems.

Use your words,	*(move four fingers forward and back in front of mouth)*
Use your words.	
When things are tough	*(pound fist over fist)*
And you shouldn't be rough,	*(bang fists side to side)*
Just use your words.	*(move four fingers forward and back in front of mouth)*

Using Manners

Sing to the tune of "Are You Sleeping."

Please and thank you,
Please and thank you,
Excuse me, excuse me.
That was very well done.
You work very nicely.
Use nice words. Use nice words.

Taking Turns

When you notice someone being good, sing this song. Put the child's name in the blank and sing to the tune of "London Bridge."

I see _____ taking turns, taking turns, taking turns.
I see _____ taking turns,
Good job _____!
(Other verses: I see/hear _____ sharing toys, using words, saying please, following rules, playing fair, etc.)

Jack and Jill

Here is a simple finger play for a familiar rhyme. Hooking index fingers both ways is American Sign Language for friends.

Jack and Jill went up the hill
> *(hook index fingers one way and the other; make a hill shape with hand)*

To fetch a pail of water.
> *(swing pail back, forth, and around head)*

Jack fell down
> *(hook index fingers one way, then swipe both hands sideways)*

And broke his crown.
> *(rubs head)*

And Jill came tumbling after.
> *(hook index fingers and roll hands and arms around)*

Copy, Color, and cut out. Use a stick puppets.

Good-Bye Songs

I'm Glad We Were Together

This is a very versatile song. You may have the children sing with you until you get to the part that is different each day (lines four and five).

I'm glad we were together, together, together. (*point to self then spread arms out for a big hug—bring arms in three times*)

I'm glad we were together. (*point to self then spread arms out for a big hug*)

We had a good day. (*arms overhead like a sun*)
We played and painted; and puzzled and measured.
We learned about seven and read about dinosaurs. (*Fill in your own activities here. The list can be as short or as long as you can keep it up.*)

I'm glad we were together. We had so much fun.

It's time to say good-bye now, good-bye now, good-bye now. (*wave good-bye*)
It's time to say good-bye now. (*wave good-bye*)
Best wishes to you. (*touch heart and thumbs up*)

I'll see you all on Monday, on Monday, on Monday. (*use correct day*)
I'll see you all on Monday,
When we'll work again.

How Will You Get Home Today?

How will you get home today?
How will you get home?
Do you take the bus?
Do you walk home on your own?
Do you ride your bike?
Do you ride in a car?
Do you take the train?
Is your house very far?
Do you ride a camel?
Do you lead a yak?
Do you take the space shuttle?
How long till you get back?
How will you get home today?
By scooter, car, or friend?
Whatever way is best for you,
Be safe till I see you again.

Groundhogs

Groundhog's Day

Is it difficult to remember what the shadow means for winter? This rhyme will help you keep it straight.

Groundhog, groundhog,
Good morning sleepy head.
More winter if you see your shadow,
If you don't, it's spring instead.

Punxsutawney Phil

Punxsutawney Phil is the official groundhog of Groundhog's Day. In this rhyme, you can have one student lead the class on the ups and downs.

Punxsutawney Phil says jump up, it's time to wake.	*(jump up to stand)*
Go back to sleep, for a shadow I did make.	*(sit down and rest head on hand)*
Punxsutawney Phil says pop up, it's time to play.	*(jump up to stand)*
Did I see my shadow? Not today.	*(shake head and put hands up)*
Punxsutawney Phil says get up and look around.	*(hold hand over eyes and look around)*
On February 2 we look for shadows on the ground.	*(look on the ground)*

My Shadow

Take the class outside so the children can see if they cast shadows. Talk about what makes a shadow. Show the students that they stand between the sun and their shadows (when they face their shadows, the sun is behind them). Go back outside at noon and see how the shadows have changed. Talk about why the shadows change size (and direction).

Morning rhyme:
My shadow is taller than me this morning. It isn't fair.
Just wait till noon and we'll see who is bigger, if you dare.

Noon rhyme:
Now we see who's bigger, I'm the one who grew.
Just stick with me, my shadow, I'll take care of you.

Healthy Habits

Cover Your Cough

Cover your cough, cough, cough.   (pretend to cough)
Cover your sneeze, sneeze, sneeze.   (pretend to sneeze)
Use your elbow, not your hands,   (put inside of elbow over your mouth)
Keep the germs from your friends.   (wiggle fingers out from mouth)
Use a tissue, if you please, when you sneeze.   (pretend to wave a tissue and cover nose)

Nap Time

There was a young fish from Dunlap,
Who thought that he didn't need a nap.
On a day without sleep,
He wandered too deep,
And woke up on an octopus lap.

Night Light

Night light, sleep tight,
Monsters stay away tonight.
I will try with all my might
To fall asleep without my light.

Pick Your Nose

Speak in the rhythm of the tune of "Pat-a-Cake."

Pick your nose, pick your nose,   (twirl index finger in front of face)
Sneeze real loud.   (exaggerated sneeze)
Yucky nose, yucky nose,   (wiggle fingers under your nose)
Use your sleeve.   (pretend to wipe nose with your sleeve)
These are things that we won't do,   (cross arms across chest)
because if you have a cold,   (move hands back and forth and
I'll get it from you!   motion for something to come)

Wash Hands, Wash Hands

Sing to the tune of "Baa, Baa Black Sheep."
Teach this song for children to sing while they wash. Encourage them to sing the whole song before rinsing, so they wash thoroughly.

Wash hands, wash hands,
Before you eat your lunch.
Get off the paint and get off the dirt.
Lather up the soap on your fingers and your palms.
Rub your hands in back and take your time, be calm.
Wash hands, wash hands,
Rinse off all the soap.
Dry hands, dry hands, then come and eat your lunch.

Dusty Bill

Read this nursery rhyme in a crusty old cowboy voice.

I'm Dusty Bill from Vinegar Hill,
Never had a bath, and I never will.

Have your students paint the dirt on Dusty Bill. Copy and cut out Dusty Bill (below). Use brown paint on a paintbrush and a piece of screen or a sieve. When the children brush quickly on the screen over the picture, the brown paint will splatter all over, like dirt.

Hearts

Valentine for One

This valentine is for my teacher.
A bright red heart for one.
I drew a special picture
Wishing you a lot of fun.

These valentines are for Mom and Dad
Bright red hearts for two.
Giving to you makes me glad
With lots of love for you.

These valentines are for my friends
Bright red hearts for three.
I would travel the whole Earth
For good friends are we.

Valentine

Check your mailbox, don't you fret.
How many valentines did you get?
You can get one and still have fun.
You can get two and still be true.
You can get three and still be free.
You can get four and still want more.
You can get five and feel alive.
You can get six; it's just for kicks.
Valentine, you'll still be mine.

Roses Are Red

Roses are red.   (brush your index finger down your chin)
Violets are blue.   (fold thumb in palm with fingers up, shake hand)
We are best friends,   (hook index fingers one way and then the other)
And I love you.   (point to self, cross arms over chest, point to someone else)

Heart

Hearts are red   (hand on heart, brush your index finger down your chin)
Veins are blue.   (fold thumb in palm with fingers up, shake hand)
Arteries carry blood   (zig-zag your finger from heart down)
All over you.   (point to leg, head, arms)

Hello Songs

Good Morning Song

As you say this verse in a sing-song voice, encourage the children to look each other in the eyes and wave in a friendly manner to make some connections with each other. You can do this in a sing-song voice or an exuberant voice to get energy going. Develop your own style.

Teacher: Good morning   *(wave with right hand)*
Echo: Good morning   *(wave with right hand)*
Teacher: Hello   *(wave with left hand)*
Echo: Hello   *(wave with left hand)*
Teacher: Good morning   *(wave with both hands)*
Echo: Good morning   *(wave with both hands)*
All: Let's have a great day!

I'm Glad We're Here

Sing this song to the tune of "The More We Get Together" with the class as you begin circle time each morning. Be sure to sing the names in a different order each morning.

I'm glad we're here together, together, together.
    (point to self then spread arms out for a big hug—bring arms in three times)
I'm glad we're here together.
    (point to self spread arms out for a big hug)
Good morning to you.
    (fold arms in front of chest and raise right arm, keeping the elbow where it is)
Welcome to Richie and Sun and Bonnie and Ethan and Yougen and Carla,
Welcome to Sal, etc.
I'm glad we're here together.
    (point to self then spread arms out for a big hug—
    bring arms in three times)
Good morning, my friends.
    (hook index fingers one way then the opposite way)

Criss Cross Applesauce

This rhyme is short and calming for getting children settled down to listen to a story or directions.

Criss cross, applesauce   *(sit cross legged)*
Let's sit by the teacher and sing.
We'll read a book   *(hold hands like a book)*
And take a look
At every wonderful thing.   *(pretend to look through a magnifying glass)*

Pass the Light

Students pass around a hand mirror as you say this rhyme. They take a glance and pass it on. Say the name of the child who is holding the mirror as you get to that part of the rhyme. That child can hold it until the end of the poem. Repeat the rhyme several times. If you can't say the name of each child each day, try to include each child sometime during the week. It is especially nice if the mirror is shaped like a heart or star.

Pass the light for all to see.
A class of bright faces* are we.
We all have a special way to shine:
A smile, some help, a talent, some time.
Pass the light for all to see.
(Name) is shining brightly.

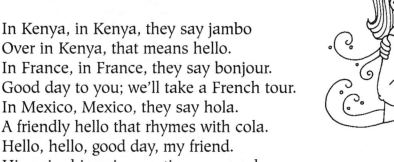

*You can substitute your own term here: group of friends, team of learners, friendly community, loving family, etc.

Hello in Four Languages

Sung to the tune of "To Market, to Market."

In Kenya, in Kenya, they say jambo
Over in Kenya, that means hello.
In France, in France, they say bonjour.
Good day to you; we'll take a French tour.
In Mexico, Mexico, they say hola.
A friendly hello that rhymes with cola.
Hello, hello, good day, my friend.
Hi again, hi again, greetings we send.

(Students walk around and try to say hello to as many other children as possible in any of the four languages practiced.)

Mail

Mailman

Sing to the tune of "Frère Jacques."

Mailman, mailman,	*(or letter carrier to be politically correct)*
Mailman, mailman,	*(arm around a mailbag, other hand holding strap)*
Bring my mail	*(hands out, palms up and together)*
To my house.	*(hands in shape of a roof)*
Put it in the mailbox.	*(motion of putting in)*
Push it through the mail slot.	*(fingers and thumbs make shape of a slot)*
I'll read it	*(hands make a book, pretend to read)*
When I'm home.	

Sending a Letter

Sing to the tune of "Have You Ever Seen a Lassie?"

How do you send a letter, a letter, a letter?
How do you send a letter?
You send it like this:
You write it and seal it and stamp it and mail it.
    (hand motions: scribble, lick, fist stamp, and put in mailbox)
How do you send a letter to friends far away?

What happens to your letter, your letter, your letter?
What happens to your letter
At the post office?
They sort it and stamp it and fly it or drive it.
    (hand motions: hand over hand, fist stamp, hand like plane, and steering wheel)
They put it in the mailbox of friends far away.

Early in the Morning

Here's a finger play for a traditional rhyme.

Early in the morning at eight o'clock	*(left fingers inside right elbow; right palm up; raise right arm straight up; show eight fingers)*
You can hear the postman's knock;	*(knock on imaginary door)*
Up jumps Ella to answer the door,	*(lift hands, palms up; bring palms together and open like a door)*
One letter, two letters, three letters, four!	*(count on four fingers)*

Math

Patterns

Pattern, pattern, clap with me.   (clap with words)
Clap clap, march march, one two three.   (clap and march with words)
Clap, clap up   (clap with hands over heads)
March, march down   (marching feet)
Clap and march all over town.   (clap and march around circle)

Doubles

Say this as a call-and-response rhyme. One group says the first part, and the other group calls the rhyming part.

One and one is two—Tie your shoe!
Two and two is four—Close the door!
Three and three is six—Pick up sticks!
Four and four is eight—Lay them straight!
Five and five is ten—Let's do it again!
Six and six is twelve—Put it on the shelf!
Seven and seven is fourteen—You are clean!
Eight and eight is sixteen—You are green!
Nine and nine is eighteen—You're an adding machine!

One for Sorrow

This is a traditional Mother Goose rhyme.

One for sorrow   (fingers pull down corners of lips)
Two for joy   (open palms at side of face)
Three for a girl   (point to any girl)
Four for a boy   (point to any boy)
Five for silver   (pick up an imaginary pile of money from one palm and drop it, repeat)
Six for gold   (show off rings and necklace)
Seven for a secret   (finger at lips)
Ne'er to be told.   (cover mouth and shake head)

Movement and Motion

Let's Move!

Sung to the tune of "Mulberry Bush" while you march in a large circle.

We are marching 'round and 'round,
'round and 'round, 'round and 'round.
We are marching 'round and 'round.
Let's have a class parade.

Sing other verses substituting a different movement for marching (skipping, running, prancing, sliding, scurrying).

You Gotta Dance

Students do whatever "the spirit" is telling them to do.

You gotta dance when the spirit says dance.
You gotta dance when the spirit says dance.
When the spirit says dance, you gotta dance right along.
Dance when the spirit says dance.

Substitute other words for dance: skip, hop, clap, kick, stomp.

Preschool Train

This can be chanted. The students pretend to ride, march, and dance to the beat.

We're riding in the preschool train.
We're riding in the preschool train.
It's the same old train that brought us here,
And it's gonna bring us back again.

We're marching in the big parade.
We're marching in the big parade.
It's the holiday parade that we all love,
And we're playing tunes that we made.

We're dancing in the kid's ballet.
We're dancing in the kid's ballet.
We love to dance and raise our arms.
Watch us as we kick, twirl, and sway.

Night and Day

Hey Diddle, Diddle

Hey diddle, diddle!　　　　　　　*(wave your hand above your head)*

The cat and the fiddle　　　　　　*(pull a whisker from your face with your thumb and index finger, then pretend to play a violin)*

The cow jumped over the moon.　　*(put your thumb where a horn would be on your head and twist your hand forward)*

The little dog laughed to see such sport,　*(snap your fingers and tap your leg)*

And the dish ran away with the spoon.　*(put your thumbs together in front of your chest; as you wiggle your index fingers, move your hands forward)*

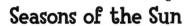

Seasons of the Sun
Sung to the tune of "London Bridge."

Summer sun is shining down,　　　　*(bring a crooked finger across your forehead)*

Shining down, shining down.　　　　*(bring fingers down in sunbursts)*

Summer sun is shining down

On the kids and flowers.　　　　　　*(touch fingers on one side of nose and bring them around to the other side)*

Autumn sun is shining down,　　　　*(arms in circle above head)*

Shining down, shining down.　　　　*(bring fingers down in sunbursts)*

Autumn sun is shining down

On cool, colored leaves.　　　　　　*(flap your hand from the wrist while pointing to the wrist with the other index finger)*

Winter sun, come out to play,　　　　*(make open fingers flutter down)*

Out to play, out to play.　　　　　　*(stick out pinkies and thumbs and twist)*

Winter sun, come out to play,

Don't hide behind the clouds.　　　　*(hold arm over eyes)*

Springtime sun we welcome you,　　　*(arms in circle above head)*

Welcome you, welcome you.　　　　　*(welcoming gesture)*

Springtime sun, we welcome you

With rainbows and spring showers.　　*(wave your open hands down)*

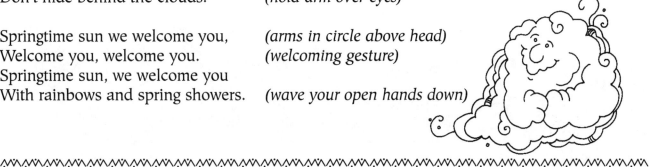

The Evening Is Coming

By anonymous

The evening is coming. The sun sinks to rest.
>*(bring cupped hand down from shoulder to rest on the back of your other hand)*

The birds are all flying straight home to their nests.
>*(fly arms)*

"Caw, caw," says the crow as he flies overhead.
>*(cup hands around mouth)*

It's time little children were going to bed.
>*(make a pillow with your hands and rest your cheek on them)*

Here comes the pony. Her work is all done.
>*(straddle an upside-down V on the opposite hand and bounce)*

Down through the meadow she takes a good run.
>*(make thumbs touch; wiggle index fingers, move forward)*

Up go her heels, and down goes her head.
>*(bring head down/heel up)*

It's time little children were going to bed.
>*(make a pillow with your hands and rest your cheek on them)*

The Moon

The moon glows brightly in the night
>*(cup your hand in the air and bring it down slowly to rest—still cupped—on the back of the other hand)*

When the sun sinks low.
>*(form a letter c with your finger and thumb; tap it around your eye)*

I like to wonder when it's half
>*(hold one hand straight and cup the other palm to palm)*

Will it shrink or grow?
>*(flatten hands palm to palm; then round into ball)*

The Waning and Waxing Moon

Sung to the tune of "The Farmer in the Dell."

The moon is full and round.   *(make a round shape with hands)*
The moon is full and round.
One night a month, the moon looks full.
The moon is full and round.

The moon is waning now.   *(cup your left hand)*
The moon is waning now.
Cradle the moon in your left hand.
It wanes down to a band.

The moon we cannot see.   *(pretend to look for the moon)*
The moon we cannot see.
One time a month, the moon is new.
The moon we cannot see.

The moon is waxing now.   *(cup your right hand)*
The moon is waxing now.
Hold the moon tight in your right.
And watch it grow each night.

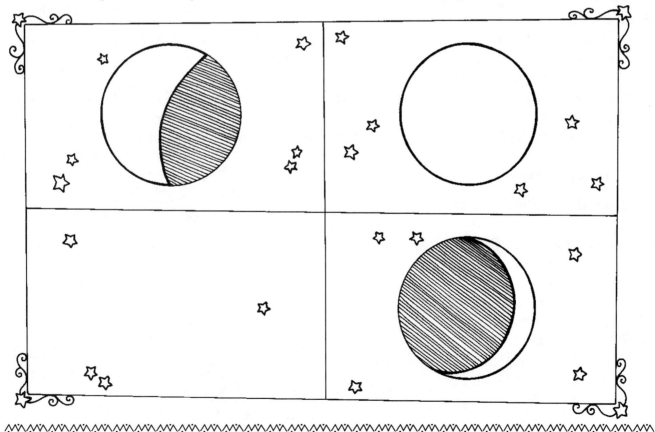

Nursery Rhymes

Each Peach, Pear, Plum

Snap your fingers, beat the drum. Use the nursery rhyme characters on pages 51 and 52 to create mini-books.

Mother Goose take a break
See what rhymes we can make.
Michael, row your boat ashore.
Aren't your arms feeling sore?
Little Boy Blue wake up; it's late.
Get back home and lock the gate.
Yankee Doodle, lose that hat!
Noodles for lunch, not like that!
Little Jack, don't use your thumb!
Use your fork to eat that plum.
Hey diddle, diddle and fiddle-de-dee,
Mother Goose is back from tea.

Hickory, Dickory, Dock

Hickory, dickory, dock.
    (make fists with thumbs up—alternate up and down with each word)
The mouse ran up the clock.   *(run fingers up arm)*
The clock struck one.   *(hold up one finger)*
The mouse ran down.   *(run fingers down arm)*
Hickory, dickory, dock.
    (make fists with thumbs up—alternate up and down with each word)

Jell-O on a Plate

Have the children act like the food in each verse.

Jell-O on a plate, Jell-O on a plate,
Wibble, wobble, wibble wobble,
Jell-O on a plate.
Sausage in a pan, sausage in a pan,
Frizzle, frazzle, frizzle, frazzle,
Sausage in a pan.
Ice cream in a cone, ice cream in a cone,
Dribble, bibble, dribble, bibble,
Ice cream in a cone.

Follow the directions on page 50.

Mother Goose take a break.
See what rhymes we can make.

Michael, row your boat ashore.
Aren't your arms feeling sore?

Little Boy Blue wake up; it's late.
Get back home and lock the gate.

Nursery Rhyme Patterns

Follow the directions on page 50.

Yankee Doodle, lose that hat!
Noodles for lunch, not like that!

Little Jack, don't use your thumb!
Use your fork to eat that plum.

Hey diddle, diddle and fiddle-de dee,
Mother Goose is back from tea.

Pets

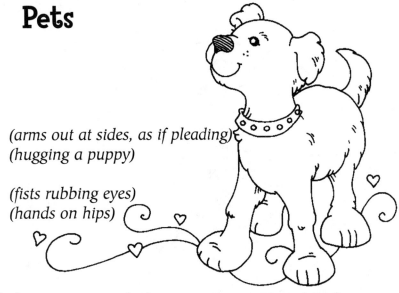

Puppy

Sung to the tune of "Jack and Jill."

Mom and Dad, please let me keep
This puppy I have met.
He needs a home,
I'm all alone,
I'll be in charge of my pet.

(arms out at sides, as if pleading)
(hugging a puppy)

(fists rubbing eyes)
(hands on hips)

Six Little Kittens

This counting rhyme can be done with fingers, or copy the kittens on pages 53 and 54 for puppets or a simple mini-book.

Six little kittens glad to be alive. One saw a mouse and then there were five.
Five little kittens rolled on the floor. One found some yarn and then there were four.
Four little kittens climbing on a tree. One spied a bird and then there were three.
Three little kittens eating fish stew. One took a nap and then there were two.
Two little kittens playing in the sun. One chased a butterfly and then there was one.
One little kitten yawned and rubbed his eyes. Heard a quiet noise and five kittens say, "Surprise!"
Six happy kittens playing stalk and creep. Played all day . . . and now they're all asleep.

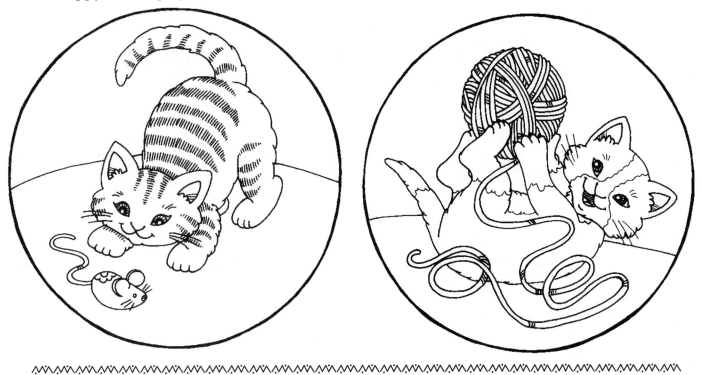

Directions are found on page 53.

Skip to My Lou

This is an easy song to adapt to any theme. Just think of lots of words that rhyme with lou. Usually the song is about things going wrong.

Chorus:
Skip, skip, skip to my lou.
Skip, skip, skip to my lou.
Skip, skip, skip to my lou.
Skip to my lou, my darling.

Bird's in the bathroom, whistling a tune.
Cat's in the baby's room, snuggling with Drew.
Dog's in the pantry, honest, it's true.
Skip to my lou, my darling.

Hamster's in the sneaker, need a new shoe.
Snake's in the chimney, blocking the flue.
Snail's in the bathtub, stuck like glue.
Skip to my lou, my darling.

Cow's in the kitchen, singing out moo.
Lizard's in the arm chair, that was just new.
Horse's in the window, blocking the view.
Skip to my lou, my darling.

Animals in the attic, what'll I do?
The house is crowded, what a zoo.
Pets on parade, it's a hullaballou.
Skip to my lou, my darling.

Old Mother Hubbard

The children can make up their own additions to the food Mother Hubbard went to buy and the silly things the dog did. This would make a cute class book with illustrations.

Old Mother Hubbard went to the cupboard,   *(open cupboard doors)*
To fetch her poor dog a bone;   *(begging hands)*
But when she got there,
The cupboard was bare   *(shrug with hands up)*
And so the poor dog had none.   *(make a zero with index finger and thumb)*

She went to the dock, to buy him some fish
But when she got back, he was eating his dish.

She went to the bakers to buy him some bread
But when she got back, he was lying in bed.

She went to the market to buy him some fruit
But when she got back, he was eating a boot.

She went to the dairy to buy him some milk
But when she got back, he was spinning some silk.

Nine Little Fishes

Sing to the tune of "Ten Little Indians" and count on your fingers.

One little, two little, three little fishes,
Four little, five little, six little fishes,
Seven little, eight little, nine little fishes,
Swimming in the tank.

Count with Me

Copy the cards on page 57 and cut them out. Give the children copies of the cards to hold up as you say the poem.

I have two cats at my house;   *(pull whiskers)*
They get along fine with my one little mouse.   *(wrinkle nose and wiggle fingers for whiskers)*
In a tank, I have four fish   *(hands together swish like a fish)*
Who are never aware of the dog with a wish.   *(begging hands)*
And in a cage in my room   *(make a box with flat hands)*
Two ferrets run and primly groom.   *(pretend to lick hands)*
Do you think that's a lot?
That's how many pets I have got.

Count with Me

Follow the directions on page 56.

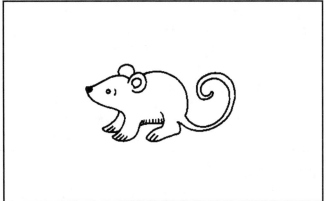

Pumpkins

Peter, the Pumpkin Grower

Peter, Peter, pumpkin grower
Had a field and loved to show her.
Peter's were the best I hear.
He always won first prize each year.

Pumpkins

Sung to the tune of "Pop! Goes the Weasel."

All around the pumpkin patch   (spin finger pointing down)
Are round and fat and tall ones.   (make hands round and tall)
The pumpkins growing in the sun,   (make a sun over your head)
Splat, there's a flat one!   (clap your hands together horizontally)

Five Spooky Pumpkins

After you say the line, do the action and words in ( ) with the children. This can be used with puppets or felt pumpkins.

Five spooky pumpkins on the stair,   (count on five fingers)
We worked all night for a scare.   (say "boo")
When the goblins came by   (creep fingers and knock on a door)
Our looks made them shy;   (hide eyes shyly)
Blow out my candle if you dare.   (blow on tip of index finger)

Four spooky pumpkins on the stair,   (count on four fingers)
We worked all night for a scare.   (say "boo")
When the witches came by   (creep fingers and knock on door)
Our looks made them shy;   (hide eyes shyly)
Blow out my candle if you dare.   (blow on tip of index finger)

Three spooky pumpkins on the stair,   (count on three fingers)
We worked all night for a scare.   (say "boo")
When the ghosts came by   (creep fingers and knock on door)
Our looks made them shy;   (hide eyes shyly)
Blow out my candle if you dare.   (blow on tip of index finger)

Two spooky pumpkins on the stair,   (count on two fingers)
We worked all night for a scare.   (say "boo")
When the puppies came by   (creep fingers and knock on door)
Our looks made them shy;   (hide eyes shyly)
Blow out my candle if you dare.   (blow on tip of index finger)

One spooky pumpkin on the stair,   (count on one finger)
I worked all night for a scare.   (say "boo")
When the princess came by   (creep fingers and knock on door)
My looks made her shy;   (hide eyes shyly)
Blow out my candle if you dare.   (blow on tip of index finger)

Pumpkins

Many people do science experiments with pumpkins in the fall. Sing about what you are exploring by changing the words to this song. In subsequent verses, change "smelled" to felt, measured, weighed, lifted, counted pumpkin seeds, tasted, etc. Sing to the tune of "Have You Ever Seen a Lassie?"

Have you ever smelled a pumpkin, a pumpkin, a pumpkin?
Have you ever smelled a pumpkin
When it's harvest time?

Pumpkin Pie

Pumpkin, pumpkin, I watched you
In my garden as you grew
From green to orange, what a feat!
Now as pie you'll be a treat.

Routines

Washing Hands

Wash hands, wash;   *(rub hands together)*
Scrub backs and in between.   *(wipe backs of hands and between fingers)*
If you want to have a snack,   *(pretend to eat)*
Then wash your hands clean.   *(show clean open hands)*

Toothbrush Rhymes

Get your toothbrush, there's no rush.
Sing a song while you brush
Tiny circles, one time through.
Brush your tongue and spit the goo!

Brush, brush, brush your teeth
Tiny circles, nice and neat.
Inside up, inside down,
Outside teeth all around.
Get the tops and brush your tongue.
Brush and floss for nice, strong gums.

Shake Your Hands

This rhyme is a loud-to-quiet rhyme, which is great for the times you need to calm the group down before starting a quiet activity.

Shake your hands over your head.   *(Do the actions given in each line)*
Point to something that's red.
Wiggle your toes.
Touch your nose
And put your sillies to bed.   *(hands on lap)*

Getting Ready

Use this rhyme when you want the students to listen to directions before touching what is in front of them. When everyone has their antlers on, you can start the rhyme.

Here are moose's antlers.   (make antlers on your head)
Give the moose a tap.   (hands tap alternate shoulders)
Now we take our hands   (fold hands)
And put them in our lap.   (put hands in lap)
Wash the dishes,
Wash the dishes.   (fists rotate around each other)
Wipe the dishes,   (rub hands)
Ring the bell for tea.   (pretend to ring a bell)
Three good wishes,   (tap heart three times)
Three good kisses,   (touch lips three times)
I will give to thee.   (point to self and someone else)

Time to Listen

Now it's time to listen.
Time to play is done;
It's your time to listen.
Circle time has begun.

Clean Up Time

Sung to the tune of "Pop Goes the Weasel."

Put away the puzzles and blocks,
Put away the farm house,
Clean up the spills and trash,
We all work together.
Cleaning up is lots of fun
When we work together.
Everybody lends a hand.
Wow! The room is ready.

Five More Minutes

Bang the drum, rum, tum, tum.
Five more minutes till play is done.
Bang the drum, rum, tum, tum.
Join me and then we'll have some fun.

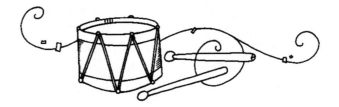

Science

Sink and Float

As you are exploring sink and float, teach the children this song. Then, as they play with different objects in the water, they can make up their own verses. Sing to the tune of "The Wheels on the Bus."

The boat in the water goes float, float, float,
float, float, float,
float, float, float.
The boat in the water goes float, float, float
In the calm blue sea.

The rock in the water goes sink, sink, sink,
sink, sink, sink,
sink, sink, sink.
The rock in the water goes sink, sink, sink
In the calm blue sea.

Using Your Senses

Sung to the tune of "The Farmer in the Dell."

My eyes help me see.
My eyes help me see.
We use our eyes
For color and size;
My eyes help me see.

My ears help me hear.
My ears help me hear.
Sounds high or low
Or loud or soft;
My ears help me hear.

My hands help me feel.
My hands help me feel.
Touch worm or trees,
Feel hot or breeze;
My hands help me feel.

My mouth helps me taste.
My mouth helps me taste.
Sweet and salty,
Sour and bitter;
My mouth helps me taste.

My nose helps me smell.
My nose helps me smell.
Flowers and bread,
Skunks and garbage;
My nose helps me smell.

Shapes

Shapes

A circle is a simple shape,
It goes 'round and 'round.
On a ball, plate, or clock,
A circle can be found.

An oval is like a circle but it can be flat or tall.
Imagine that some air is leaking out of a ball.

A square has four sides,
Each side it is the same.
Search for squares around you.
We'll play the I-spy game.

Look around and you will see
Triangles with corners three.
Three sides made a shape.
Down, over, and close the gate.

A rectangle is like a square
But the sides are not fair.
Two are short and two are long.
Even sides make it strong.
Or . . .
Two are long and two are short.
Stand them up and make a fort.

Who cut the top off my triangle?
Was it Sue, Eric, or Floyd?
Now my perfect triangle
Has become a trapezoid.

A green light says go,
A yellow light says slow,
But when a red sign says STOP,
It's an octagon, I know.

Television

No TV for Me Today

Five sleepy children watching TV all day. Mother came in and said, "Go out and play!"
Pete found a puzzle lying on his bed. He wandered off and this is what he said,
"No TV for me today, I found something much more fun to play."
Four sleepy children watching TV all day. Father came in and said, "Go out and play!"
Doris found four dolls waiting for their tea. She wandered off to play family.
"No TV for me today, I found something much more fun to play."
Three sleepy children watching TV all day. Mother came in and said, "Go out and play!"
Freddy found a baseball hiding in a mitt. He wandered off and tried to get a hit.
"No TV for me today, I found something much more fun to play."
Two sleepy children watching TV all day. Father came in and said, "Go out and play!"
Felicia found some crayons and a coloring book. She wandered off backward and didn't look.
"No TV for me today, I found something much more fun to play."
One sleepy child watching TV all day. Mother came in and said, "Go out and play!"
Lizzy found a friend playing in the sand. She wandered off and gave her friend a hand.
"No TV for me today, I found something much more fun to play."
Five laughing children, playing and having fun. Mom and Dad now knew that TV time was done!
"No TV for us today. We found something much more fun to play."

Ten Reasons to Turn Off the TV:

Read a good book.
For a bug, take a look.
Make a crunchy snack.
With couch cushions, build a shack.
Read a magazine.
Color a glittery scene.
Build some towers.
Pretend you have magic powers.
Have a daydream.
Eat some ice cream.

Transportation

Airplane

Sung to the tune of "Twinkle, Twinkle."

Airplane, airplane in the sky   *(right hand moving like a plane in the air)*
How I love to watch you fly.   *(right hand shading eyes while looking up)*
Up above our house you glide   *(pointing up)*
In between the clouds you slide.   *(pointer finger zooms across)*
Airplane, airplane o'er the trees,   *(palms together, fingers up—open up and spread apart)*
Take me with you next time, please.   *(hug body with arms)*

Getting Around

Sung to the tune of "The Wheels on the Bus." Copy and cut out the transportation cards on page 66. Give them to children, who take turns being different vehicles.

The bus on the road goes beep, beep, beep,   *(honk horn with hand)*
beep, beep, beep,
beep, beep, beep.
The bus on the road goes beep, beep, beep,
All around the world.
The plane in the air goes zoom, zoom, zoom   *(hands makes airplane wings)*
The train on the tracks goes chug a lug a lug   *(arms circle like wheels)*
The boat in the water goes toot, toot, toot   *(pull arm down from sky)*

Sailboat

Sung to the tune of "Row, Row, Row Your Boat."

Sail, sail, sail your ship
Swiftly round the sea.
See new places, hear new sounds.
That's the life for me!

Jet Airplane

Sung to the tune of "Row, Row, Row Your Boat"

Fly, fly, fly your jet
Feeling free and high.
Soaring up with birds and clouds
Racing 'cross the sky!

Down at the Station

Down at the station   *(hands make roof)*
Early in the morning   *(place hand at inside of elbow, extend arm forward and raise it up)*

See the little puffer-bellies all in a row.   *(move arms in circles at sides, tap palm with opposite hand three times in a row)*

See the engine driver   *(put on imaginary hat)*
Pull his little lever   *(hold up fist, pull down twice)*
Puff puff, peep peep, off we go.   *(move arms in circles and start marching forward)*

Transportation Cards

Follow the directions on page 65.

Turkeys

November's Scare

Tom, Tom, the turkey fair   *(wiggle four fingers as turkey feathers)*
Hid away for November's scare.   *(use the other hand to hide the fingers)*
The only thing young Tom won't be
Is turkey dinner for you or me.   *(rub your tummy)*

Ten Turkeys

Ten turkeys strutted across the road.
One turkey lifted its head and crowed,
Gobble, gobble, gobble, gobble.
The turkeys kept up their wobble.
As I watched them walk back to the wood,
I knew that those turkeys were feeling good.
Another Thanksgiving had passed them by,
For another year, they needn't be shy.

Five Fat Turkeys

This is a traditional finger play. Alternatively, cut five turkey shapes (using the pattern above) out of felt to use on a flannelboard and take down the turkeys as you say the verses.

Five fat turkeys are we.   *(hold up five fingers)*
We spent all night in a tree.   *(other arm is a branch for the turkeys)*
When the cook came around,   *(pretend to put on a cook's hat)*
We couldn't be found.   *(hand above eyes, looking)*
And that's why we're here, you see.   *(hold up five fingers)*

Tom Turkey came around and invited one down,   *(push down one finger)*
And now there are four in the tree.

Next verse begins with four fat turkeys. Recite the rhyme until there are no turkeys in the tree.

Vegetables/Garden

Underground

Carrots, turnips, onions, too,   *(crying with fists wiping eyes)*
Grow as beets and potatoes do.   *(fist over fist)*
Leaves growing up, roots shooting down. *(hands come together and separate as*
                                         they move up, opposite for roots)
Dig up veggies from the ground.   *(digging motion)*

Farmers' Market

Sing to the tune of "Down at the Station."

Down at the farmers' market   *(marching and raise hands*
Early in the morning,   *over head in a sunburst)*
See the fresh vegetables all in a row. *(chopping motion in a row)*
See the happy farmers   *(thumbs hooked in suspenders)*
Selling food they grow themselves.
Crunch, crunch, yum, yum   *(fists pound each other and rub tummy)*
Here we grow!   *(squat down and rise up as if growing fast)*

Planting

Digging in my garden,   *(pretend to dig with a shovel)*
Planting in the sun.   *(pretend to push seeds into the ground)*
A tiny seed's a promise   *(make a tiny circle with fingers and thumb)*
Of flowers soon to come.   *(palms together grow up and out)*
Add a little sunshine;   *(arms make a circle over your head)*
Add a little rain.   *(fingers wiggle down from overhead)*
The earth gives me a flower. *(palms together grow up and out)*
Summer's here again.   *(fan yourself with your hand)*

Pretty Little Garden

This spring-time rhyme uses American Sign Language for key words.

In a pretty little garden of yellow, pink and blue
    (close your fingers and bring them from one side of your nose around to the other)
I heard the birds sing and away they flew.
    (make a V with two fingers and open and close in front of your mouth like a beak)
Up and down the rows I love to run,
    (make your thumbs touch; as you wiggle your index fingers, move your hands forward)
While the tulips and the daisies open to the sun.
    (make a C with thumb and index finger and tap it around your eye)

Weather

Rain, Rain

While seated, children slap their legs alternately with each hand to simulate rain. Start out slowly and with each repetition of the rhyme, tap a little faster. Then, start going slower again until it is just lightly raining.

Rain, rain, go away, come again another day.

The Old Man Is Snoring

Copy page 70 and make mini-books to accompany this rhyme.

It's raining, it's pouring.	*(wave open hands down from sky)*
The old man is snoring;	*(touch thumb to forehead with open palm, then move it outward)*
He went to bed	*(form pillow with hand on side of face)*
And bumped his head	*(tap forehead with palm)*
And couldn't get up in the morning.	

(place left hand inside right elbow; extend right hand straight out and raise it up)

I'm a Little Puddle

Sung to the tune of "I'm a Little Teapot."

I'm a little puddle,
Small and brown.
After a rain, I'm all over town.
Put up your umbrella, boots stomp down.
Kick and splash me all around!

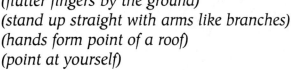

The Rain

A Mother Goose rhyme

Rain on the green grass,	*(flutter fingers by the ground)*
And rain on the tree,	*(stand up straight with arms like branches)*
And rain on the housetop,	*(hands form point of a roof)*
But not on me!	*(point at yourself)*

Snow

Snow comes twirling out of the sky,	*(twirl your body)*
Dancing snowflakes flying high.	*(dance and twirl)*
The sky is filled with gentle lace	*(twirl and wiggle fingers around)*
Drifting down to find its place.	*(wiggle fingers and bring hands down)*
In cold white blankets, snowflakes lie.	*(move hands back and forth palms down)*

The Old Man Is Snoring

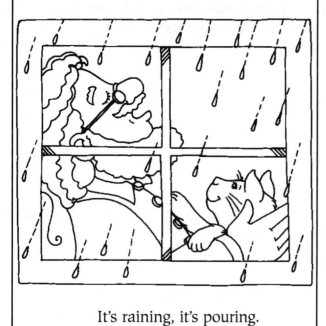

It's raining, it's pouring.

The old man is snoring;

He went to bed.
And bumped his head

And couldn't get up in the morning.

Catching Snowflakes

Sung to the tune of "BINGO."

We catch snowflakes drifting down
Catch them in your mouth-O.
Snow, snow, let it snow
Snow, snow, let it snow
Snow, snow, let it snow
Catch snowflakes in your mouth-O.

Summer Days

Sung to the tune of "Yankee Doodle."

Sunny days and bright blue skies,
We play outside all day long.
We dig in sand
And play loud games
And yell and shout and run around.
Summer days are hot and fun,
Summer days are best.
Summer days will not last long.
These summer days are blessed.

Weather

Say this rhyme each morning with your calendar. As a child picks out the symbol from page 72 that best shows today's weather, fill in the blank with the word rainy, sunny, cloudy, snowy, hot, etc.

What is the weather today, today?
What is the weather today?
I can tell by the sun
What weather we've won:
Today the weather is _____.

The Wind

A Mother Goose rhyme

The wind, the wind, the wind blows high,   (twirl finger over head)
The rain comes scattering down the sky.   (rain with fingers)

Making Bread

A Mother Goose rhyme

Blow, wind, blow!   (swish both hands around)
And go, mill, go!   (spin finger around like a windmill)
That the miller may grind the corn;   (rub fists together)
That the baker may take it, and into bread make it,   (pretend to knead)
And bring us a loaf in the morn.   (make shape of loaf with hands)

Cut apart these symbol cards and use them with the Weather rhyme on page 71.

Down by the River

Copy and cut out the circles on page 74. Staple pages together to construct mini-books to accompany this rhyme.

Down by the river in the shining sun   *(arms form a sun over head)*
There played a tabby cat with its kitten one.   *(make whiskers at mouth; show one finger)*
Purr, said the kitten,
Let's play and have fun   *(point thumbs and pinkies, twist your hands)*
While we chase butterflies in the shining sun.   *(make butterfly wings with sides of hands together; open and close palms)*

Down by the river in the water blue   *(fold thumb over palm shake hand)*
There swam a mallard with its ducklings two.   *(make a bill with a hand in front of your mouth; show two fingers)*

Quack, said the ducklings,
What shall we do   *(shrug and raise hands at sides)*
While we quack and swim in the water blue?   *(swimming motions)*

Down by the river as quiet as can be   *(finger at lips)*
Stood a gentle deer and its babies three.   *(make antlers with hands; show three fingers)*
Shhh, said the deer
What do you see   *(shade eyes with hand)*
Playing in the river as quiet as can be?   *(point thumb and pinkie; shake hand)*

Down by the river resting on the shore   *(make a pillow under your cheek with your hands)*

Sunned a water snake and its babies four.   *(bend index finger and make a spiral motion out from mouth)*

Hisss, said the snakes,
Are there any more snakes   *(shrug and raise hands at sides)*
Who are resting by the river on the shore?   *(make a pillow)*

Down by the river in a big beehive   *(make a hive shape with hands)*
There was a queen bee with her workers five.   *(show five fingers)*
Buzz! said the bees,
We're glad to be alive   *(put fingers at the corners of smiling mouth)*
As they gathered nectar for the big beehive.   *(rub tummy)*

Follow the directions on page 73.

We're Going on a Honey Hunt

This is more of a story than a finger play. Duplicate and cut apart the cards on pages 77–80 to guide the students as you go on the hunt. You may stand in place to act it out or make the hunt go around the classroom or through the halls and around the building. To make it more elaborate, decorate stations to look like the sites in the story.

All: *(chorus)* We're going on a honey hunt;
We're going to follow a bee.
It's a beautiful day
And we love honey!

Teacher: Oh, oh, a street, a busy, noisy street.
    All: We can't go over it. We can't go under it. *(palm down, hand goes over and under)*
        We'll have to go across it. *(palm down, hand goes straight out)*
    All: walk, walk, walk, walk *(look both ways, then walk in place with arms swinging)*

    All: *(chorus)*
Teacher: Oh, oh, a meadow, a tall, grassy meadow.
    All: We can't go over it. We can't go under it. *(palm down, hand goes over and under)*
        We'll have to go through it. *(palm down, hand goes straight out)*
    All: swish, scratch, swish, scratch, swish scratch *(some kids swish arms like tall grass and others scratch their legs)*

    All: *(chorus)*
Teacher: Oh, oh, a beach, a stony, hot beach.
    All: We can't go over it. We can't go under it. *(palm down, hand goes over and under)*
        We'll have to go across it. *(palm down, hand goes straight out)*
    All: ooch, ouch, ooch, ouch, ooch, ouch *(tip-toe over hot sand and sharp rocks)*

    All: *(chorus)*
Teacher: Oh, oh, a swamp, a gooey, muddy swamp.
    All: We can't go over it. We can't go under it. *(palm down, hand goes over and under)*
        We'll have to go through it. *(palm down, hand goes straight out)*
    All: ooey, gooey, ooey, gooey, ooey, gooey *(pretend to have a hard time lifting feet out of mud)*

    All: *(chorus)*
Teacher: Oh, oh, a tunnel, a narrow, dark tunnel.
    All: We can't go over it. We can't go under it. *(palm down, hand goes over and under)*
        We'll have to go through it. *(palm down, hand goes straight out)*
    All: crawl, creep, crawl, creep, crawl, creep *(crawl on hands and knees)*

All: *(chorus)*
Teacher: Oh, oh, a forest, a thick, dark forest.
All: We can't go over it. We can't go under it. *(palm down, hand goes over and under)*
We'll have to go through it. *(palm down, hand goes straight out)*
All: crunch, snap, crunch, snap, crunch, snap *(walk carefully and push branches aside)*

All: *(chorus)*
Teacher: There it is! A honey tree, a sweet, dripping honey tree.
All: Let's get some honey
All: slurp, smack, slurp, smack, slurp, smack *(pretend to eat honey)*
Teacher: Oh, oh, here come the bees.
Quick, let's get back home.
Teacher: Back through the forest! *(show cards as you go back)*
All: crunch, snap, crunch, snap, crunch, snap *(walk carefully and push branches aside)*

Teacher: Back through the tunnel!
All: crawl, creep, crawl, creep, crawl, creep *(crawl on hands and knees)*
Teacher: Back through the muddy swamp!
All: ooey, gooey, ooey, gooey, ooey, gooey *(pretend to have a hard time lifting feet out of mud)*

Teacher: Back across the beach!
All: ooch, ouch, ooch, ouch, ooch, ouch *(tip-toe over hot sand and sharp rocks)*
Teacher: Back through the meadow!
All: swish, scratch, swish, scratch, swish scratch *(some kids swish arms like tall grass and others scratch their legs)*

Teacher Back across the street!
All: walk, walk, walk, walk *(look both ways, then walk in place with arms swinging)*

Teacher: We made it!
All: Let's go again!